Amish Christmas Awakening

©2024 by Katie Lantz

All rights reserved. No part of this may be reproduced, distributed or transmitted in any form or by any means without prior written permission.
This is a work of fiction. Names, characters, places and incidents are a product of the author's imagination. Any resemblance to actual people, living or dead, or to businesses, events or locales is completely coincidental.

Contents

Chapter One

Chapter Two

Chapter Three

Chapter Four

Chapter Five

Chapter Six

Chapter Seven

Chapter Eight

Chapter Nine

Epilogue

Chapter One

Emma Fisher adjusted her prayer kapp, ensuring it sat just right atop her honey-blonde hair, which was neatly pulled back in a bun. She glanced at her reflection in the small mirror, noting the rosy blush on her cheeks, likely from the morning's chores. The familiar routine of feeding the chickens and milking the cows had always brought her a sense of peace, but today, a sense of unease gnawed at her.

Her parents were in favor of the match between her and a man named Joseph Miller, and they had never made any secret of that fact. Since she and Joseph began playing together as children, their parents imagined the two families joined through marriage.

The Millers believed it would be perfect if Joseph married Emma and could inherit her family's land, while the Miller farm could be passed down to Joseph's older brother, Henry. Joseph welcomed their parents' matchmaking attempts to bring him and Emma together.

Joseph was a good man, reliable and kind, with sandy hair and a warm, genuine smile that had always made her feel at ease. Yet, despite their history and the hopes of their parents, Emma couldn't summon any romantic feelings for him. Her interest lay elsewhere at the moment, and her heart fluttered with anticipation, not just for the forthcoming festive Christmas season but because she found herself becoming fascinated with the Englisch veterinarian, Dr. Ross Michaels.

Emma was lost in thought when her mother, Maria, called her from the kitchen. "Emma, can you help me with the bread?"

"Coming, Mamm," Emma replied, shaking off her daydreams. She moved quickly to the kitchen, where the comforting aroma of baking bread filled the air.

"Thank you, dear," Maria said with a warm smile. She was a petite woman with soft brown eyes and graying hair that she kept tucked under her prayer kapp. "Your daed will be in soon, and he'll be hungry."

As they worked together, kneading the dough and shaping the loaves, Maria glanced at her daughter. "You know, Emma, Joseph's parents were over yesterday. They spoke highly of you."

Emma stiffened slightly but kept her focus on the dough. "What did they say?"

Maria's smile widened. "Oh, just how wonderful it would be if you and Joseph were to marry. They think very highly of you, and so do we."

Emma nodded, feeling the familiar pressure settle over her. "I know, Mamm. Joseph is a good man, but..."

Maria placed a gentle hand on Emma's arm. "What, dear? Is there someone else?"

Emma hesitated, then decided to confide in her mother. "It's not that, exactly. It's just... I've been thinking about Dr.

Michaels." He was only here to tend the horses, and yet...

Mamm's eyes widened slightly. "The Englisch veterinarian? Emma, you know how your daed feels about getting too close to the Englisch."

"I know, Mamm," Emma said quickly. "It's not like that. I just... I admire him, that's all."

Maria's expression softened. "Admiration is one thing, Emma, but be careful. Our way of life is very different from his."

Emma nodded, though her thoughts were far from settled. She helped her mother finish the bread, then excused herself to the barn, where she found her daed, Abram, working on fixing a broken fence.

"Daed, do you need any help?" she asked, stepping into the cool shade of the barn.

He looked up, his weathered face breaking into a smile. "Emma, your timing is perfect. Hand me that hammer, will you?"

She did as he asked, watching him work with steady, practiced movements. Her daed was a strong man, tall and broad like Dr. Michaels, but with years of hard work etched into his features.

"Daed," she began hesitantly, "what do you think about Dr. Michaels?"

Abram paused, looking at her thoughtfully. "Dr. Michaels? He's a good vet. Knows his stuff. Why do you ask?"

Emma shrugged, trying to appear casual. "I just think he's interesting, that's all. He's different from anyone I've ever met."

Abram's expression grew serious. "Emma, it's natural to be curious about the Englisch, but remember, our ways are different for a reason. Your mamm and I want what's best for you. Joseph is a good man, and he understands our ways."

"I understand, Daed," Emma said quietly. "What if... what if there's something more out there for me?"

Daed sighed, setting the hammer down. "Emma, we all have our paths to follow.

Sometimes it's not easy to see the way, but we trust in Gott to guide us. Pray on it, and you'll find your answer."

Emma nodded, though her heart still felt heavy with uncertainty. She spent the rest of the afternoon tending to the animals, her thoughts drifting constantly to Dr. Michaels and the confusing feelings he stirred within her.

***

The next day, as she was finishing her chores, Emma saw a familiar figure approaching the farmhouse. Joseph Miller, with his sandy hair and warm smile, walked up the path, carrying a basket of apples. The sight of him brought a mix of emotions, a tangle of anticipation and dread.

"Morning, Emma," he called, his voice cheerful despite the chill in the air.

"Morning, Joseph," she replied, trying to muster a smile. Her heart pounded, knowing this conversation was inevitable.

"I brought these over from our orchard. Thought you might like some fresh apples for baking."

"Thank you," Emma said, taking the basket. The apples were a perfect distraction, but they couldn't ward off the conversation she knew was coming. "That's very kind of you."

Joseph hesitated, then glanced around before speaking. "Emma, can we talk for a moment?"

Emma's heart sank, knowing what was coming. She had seen the signs, felt the shift in their interactions. "Of course, Joseph. What is it?"

He shifted nervously, his eyes earnest and searching. "Emma, we've known each other for a long time. Our families have always hoped... well, you know. I... I have feelings for you, Emma. More than just friendship."

Emma looked down, her heart aching. She had hoped to have more time, to sort through her feelings without the pressure of his expectations. "Joseph, you're a wonderful man, and I care about you deeply. I just… don't feel the same way. Not right now, anyway."

Joseph's face fell, the light in his eyes dimming. He nodded, trying to hide his disappointment with a brave smile. "I understand, Emma. I just had to tell you how I feel. Maybe, in time, things will change."

"Maybe," Emma said softly, her voice thick and unsteady. "For now, I just need some time to figure things out."

Joseph gave her a small, sad smile. "Take all the time you need, Emma. I'll be here."

As he walked away, Emma felt a pang of guilt but also a sense of relief. She knew she had to follow her heart, even if it meant disappointing those she cared about. She watched Joseph until he disappeared down the path, then turned back to the farmhouse, her mind swirling with thoughts of the future and the choices she had yet to make.

The days that followed were a blur of activity. Emma tried to throw herself into her chores, but her thoughts kept drifting back to Joseph and the conversation they had shared. She couldn't shake the guilt she felt for hurting him, nor the confusion about her own feelings.

One evening, as she sat by the fire with her parents, she found herself unable to concentrate on the book in her lap. Her mother noticed her distraction and laid a gentle hand on her arm.

"Emma, are you all right?" Maria asked, her voice filled with concern.

Emma sighed, closing the book and looking into the flickering flames. "I'm just...thinking about Joseph."

Abram, who had been reading the newspaper, lowered it and glanced over. "Is something troubling you, love?"

Emma hesitated, then decided to confide in them. "Joseph told me he has feelings for me. More than just friendship."

Maria's eyes softened with understanding. "How do you feel about him?"

Emma shook her head, tears welling up in her eyes. "I don't know. He's such a good man, and I care about him, but I don't feel the same way."

Abram nodded thoughtfully. "It's important to follow your heart, Emma.

Feelings can grow in time. Joseph is a good match, and sometimes love comes after."

Maria added, "We just want you to be happy, dear. Whatever you decide, we'll support you."

Emma smiled through her tears, grateful for their support but still feeling the weight of her decision. "Thank you. I just need some time to sort things out."

The next morning, as she went about her chores, Emma couldn't help but replay the conversation with Joseph in her mind. His words, his disappointment, and his unwavering support lingered with her. She finished her work in the barn and went outside, the crisp air biting at her cheeks.

As she was gathering firewood, she saw Joseph again, this time helping her father fix a fence that had been damaged in the storm. He worked with a quiet determination, his sandy hair tousled by the wind. Emma felt a pang of something deeper than friendship—something that felt like longing.

It seemed that Joseph was there wherever she looked; at the farm, at the market, and in town.

The more she tried to avoid him, the more it seemed impossible.

Chapter Two

The days leading up to Christmas were filled with preparations and festivity. The community gathered for the annual Christmas market, and the air was filled with the scent of baked goods, the sound of laughter, and the warmth of hot cocoa. Emma tried to immerse herself in the joy of the season, but her thoughts kept returning to Dr. Michaels and the feelings he evoked in her.

Ross Michaels was so different from all the young Amish men Emma knew. He didn't treat her any differently than anyone else he encountered. She felt like he accepted her just as she was and didn't want her to change.

To be with him, she would have to live a completely different life. She couldn't imagine giving up her family, her community, and the traditions that were such a deep part of her. Nor could she see Ross joining the Amish faith. He wouldn't be able to continue using the types of technology that were necessary for his veterinarian practice or drive his truck to treat animals in the outlying countryside many miles from town.

Besides, she wasn't even sure whether his seeming interest in her stemmed from anything more than mere politeness.

One crisp afternoon, as she was tending to the horses, she heard the sound of a vehicle approaching. Her heart skipped a beat when she saw Dr. Michaels' truck pull up. He stepped out, looking as ruggedly handsome as ever, and gave her a friendly wave.

"Hello, Emma," he called, striding over to her. "How are the horses today?"

"They're doing much better, Dr. Michaels," she replied, trying to keep her voice steady. "Thank you for coming."

"Always a pleasure," he said with a smile. "Please, call me Ross."

Emma blushed, feeling a flutter of excitement. "All right, Ross."

As they worked together to check on the horses, Emma found herself drawn to his easy manner and the way he genuinely cared for the animals. They talked about the horses, the farm, and even a little about their lives. She learned that he had grown up in a small town not far from Lakewood Springs and had always loved working with animals.

"You have a real gift with them," Emma said, watching as he gently examined one of the mares.

Ross smiled, his eyes meeting hers. "Thank you, Emma. It's something I've always felt passionate about."

They finished the check-up, and as Ross packed up his equipment, he turned to her. "Emma, would you like to go for a walk? There's a beautiful trail just beyond the fields."

Emma hesitated, knowing her parents would disapprove of her spending time alone with an Englisch man. The thought of a walk with Ross was too tempting to resist.

"I'd like that," she said softly.

As they walked along the trail, the conversation flowed easily. Emma found herself opening up to Ross in a way she hadn't with anyone else. They talked about their hopes, dreams, and the challenges they faced. For the first time, Emma felt a connection that went beyond friendship or family expectations.

The trail wound through the woods, the bare branches of the trees creating a delicate latticework against the winter sky. Snow crunched under their boots, and the air was crisp and invigorating. Emma felt a strange sense of peace walking beside Ross, their footsteps syncing in a comforting rhythm.

"I've always loved your farm," Ross said after a moment, his voice breaking the serene silence. "It's so calming. Sometimes, I think it would be nice to live somewhere like this."

Emma's heart stuttered. "O-oh?"

"Mm. Of course, it would be incredibly impractical. Even so, I like to imagine it."

Emma glanced at him, trying to gauge his expression. He looked thoughtful, his eyes taking in the scenery around them. The path they were on curved gently, leading them past a small, frozen stream. The water beneath the ice was still and clear, reflecting the overcast sky like a mirror.

"What do you imagine?" Emma asked, her curiosity piqued.

Ross smiled, a distant look in his eyes. "I imagine waking up early, like you do, tending to the animals, feeling the earth under my hands. There's something so honest about farm work. It's grounding."

Emma nodded, understanding exactly what he meant. "It is. There's a rhythm to it, a connection to the land and the seasons. It makes you appreciate the small things."

Ross looked at her, his gaze warm and appreciative. "You're lucky, Emma. To have this place, this life. It's a gift."

She smiled, feeling a flush of warmth despite the cold. "I suppose I am. It's not always easy. There's a lot of hard work, and it can be isolating sometimes."

"True," Ross agreed. "There's also a beauty in that simplicity. In knowing that what you're doing matters, that it's real."

Emma felt a pang of something—longing, perhaps? She wasn't sure. As they looped around the big oak tree that stood sentinel at the edge of the field, she let herself imagine what it would be like if Ross were a part of this life. She pictured him working alongside her father, sharing meals with her family, and sitting on the porch in the afternoons, watching the sun set over the fields.

The image was so vivid, so appealing, that it made her heart ache. She had never allowed herself to think of a future that included Ross in such a way, but now that the thought was there, it was hard to push aside.

"I think you'd be good at it," she said quietly. "Living on a farm, I mean. You have a way with animals."

Ross chuckled, a deep, pleasant sound that made Emma's heart flutter. "Thanks, Emma. That means a lot, coming from you."

They walked in comfortable silence for a while, each lost in their own thoughts. The path led them through a grove of evergreens, their branches heavy with snow. The air smelled fresh and clean, and the quiet of the woods was soothing.

"I've always admired your dedication," Ross said suddenly, his voice soft. "The way you take care of your family, your home. It's inspiring."

Emma felt a blush creep up her cheeks. "Thank you."

He glanced at her, his eyes serious. "I mean it, Emma. You're remarkable."

Her blush deepened, and she looked away, feeling both flattered and shy. They continued walking, the farmhouse coming into view as they emerged from the woods. The sight of it, nestled against the backdrop of snow-covered fields, filled Emma with a sense of belonging and pride.

As they approached the farmhouse, Ross slowed his pace. "I guess this is where we part ways. The driveway is just on the other side of these trees."

Emma nodded, feeling a twinge of disappointment. "Thank you for the walk. It was nice to talk."

Ross smiled, his eyes lingering on her face. "It was. I hope we can do it again sometime."

Emma returned his smile, feeling a warmth spread through her. "I'd like that."

They stood there for a moment, the cold air swirling around them, neither wanting to end the moment. Finally, Ross reached out and gently squeezed her hand. "Take care, Emma."

"You too, Ross," she replied, her voice soft.

She watched as he turned and vanished through the trees to the road, his figure gradually blending into the winter landscape. Emma stood there for a while, her mind buzzing with the possibilities that had been sparked by their conversation.

When Emma returned to the farmhouse, her parents were waiting for her.

The warm, comforting aroma of a freshly baked pie filled the kitchen, but the atmosphere was tense. Abram looked at her with a serious expression. "Emma, we need to talk."

Emma sat down at the kitchen table, her heart heavy with apprehension. The fire crackled in the hearth, casting flickering shadows on the walls. "What is it, Daed?"

"We spoke to Joseph's parents earlier this week," Abram began, his voice steady but laced with concern. "They're very eager for you and Joseph to marry. We think it's a good match. You've known each other for so long, and we believe that love will grow from friendship if you open your heart to the possibility."

Maria nodded in agreement, her eyes filled with a mixture of hope and worry. "We understand that you might have feelings for Dr. Michaels, but he's an Englischer. We don't want you to leave our faith, Emma. Our way of life is important, and we believe Joseph is the right person for you."

Emma felt a pang of guilt and confusion. She knew her parents only wanted what was best for her, but her heart was torn. "I understand, Mamm, Daed. It's not that simple. I care about Ross, and he makes me feel...different."

Abram reached out and took her hand, his grip firm and reassuring. "We just want you to consider what's best for your future, Emma. Joseph is a good man, and he understands our ways. Dr. Michaels, as kind as he may be, comes from a different world. We worry about what that would mean for you."

Emma nodded, tears welling up in her eyes. "I know you're right. I… need some time to think. I need to figure out what's in my heart."

Maria squeezed her hand gently, her touch comforting but her eyes serious. "Take the time you need, Emma. We trust you to make the right decision."

Emma felt the weight of their expectations pressing down on her. She knew her parents loved her and wanted her to be happy, but the thought of disappointing them was almost unbearable. She looked at her father, his weathered face etched with concern, and her mother, whose eyes held both love and worry.

"Daed, Mamm," she began, her voice trembling, "I've always tried to do what's right by our family and our community. I've always respected our ways, but this decision... it feels so much bigger than anything I've faced before."

Abram's expression softened, and he leaned in closer. "We know, Emma. And we don't want to rush you. You have to understand that Joseph is a part of our world. He shares our values, our faith. Dr. Michaels, as good a man as he is, doesn't."

Maria nodded, her gaze steady. "We don't want to lose you, Emma. If you choose to be with the kind doctor, it could mean leaving behind everything you've known."

Emma's heart ached with the truth of their words. She loved her family, her community, and the simple, steadfast life they led. Ross had awakened something in her, a longing for something different, something more.

"I just need some time," she said again, her voice barely above a whisper.

Abram patted her hand, his touch warm and reassuring. "We understand, Emma. Take the time you need, but remember what's at stake."

Emma nodded, rising from the table. She felt the need for fresh air, for space to think. She wrapped her shawl tightly around her shoulders and stepped out into the cold evening. The stars were beginning to appear, twinkling in the clear winter sky.

She walked slowly, her thoughts a whirlwind. She thought about Joseph, his steady presence and kind heart. She had known him for so long, and he had always been there for her. When she thought about Ross, her heart beat faster. His passion for his work, his gentle nature, and the way he made her feel seen and appreciated in a way no one else had ever done stirred something deep within her.

As she wandered through the snow-covered fields, she prayed silently for guidance. "Gott, please show me the way. Help me to understand what is in my heart and what path I should take."

The night was still, the only sound the crunch of her footsteps in the snow. She knew she had to make a decision soon, but the thought of choosing between her family's expectations and her own desires was daunting.

Returning to the farmhouse, she saw the warm light spilling out from the windows. She paused, looking at the home she loved, the life she cherished. Could she really leave it all behind for a chance at something uncertain with Ross? Yet, could she ignore the feelings he stirred in her heart?

As she stepped back inside, Maria looked up from her knitting, her eyes filled with understanding. "Did you get some clarity, dear?"

Emma shook her head, a small smile tugging at her lips. "Not yet, Mamm. I'm praying for it."

Maria nodded, her expression softening. "Well, that's a start."

Abram added, "Just remember, we want you to be happy. Truly happy."

Emma nodded, tears prickling at her eyes again. "I know."

She also knew the road ahead was uncertain, but she took comfort in the fact that her family was behind her. She needed to find a way to balance her own happiness with the expectations of those she loved. In time, she hoped, she would find the path that was right for her.

As she climbed the stairs to her room, Emma's mind continued to whirl with thoughts of Joseph and Ross. She couldn't help but think of the walk she had taken with

Ross earlier that day. The way he spoke about the farm, the sincerity in his eyes—it had touched her deeply. She found herself replaying their conversation, wondering what it would be like if he truly became a part of her life.

Entering her room, she sat down at her small wooden desk and pulled out a piece of paper and a pen. Writing had always helped her organize her thoughts. She began to jot down her feelings, her hopes, and her fears. The act of writing brought a sense of clarity, and she found herself reflecting on the qualities she admired in both men.

Joseph was steady, kind, and reliable. He shared her values and her way of life. She knew he would make a wonderful husband and partner. But with Ross, there was a spark, an excitement she hadn't felt before. He saw the world differently, and being with him made her feel alive in a way she couldn't quite explain.

She wrote about her fears of leaving her community and the life she had always known. Could she truly be happy in a world so different from her own? What about Ross? Would he be willing to embrace her way of life if it came to that?

The questions seemed endless, but as she wrote, she felt a sense of peace begin to settle over her. She didn't have all the answers yet, but she was beginning to understand her own heart a little better.

After a while, she folded the paper and placed it in her Bible, a symbol of her trust in Gott's guidance. She knelt by her bed, praying once more for wisdom and clarity. "Gott, please help me to see the path you have laid out for me. Give me the strength to follow it, no matter where it leads."

Rising from her prayer, she felt a renewed sense of calm. She knew the decision wouldn't be easy, but she was determined to face it with courage and faith.

Chapter Three

Joseph watched Emma from a distance, his heart aching with the familiar blend of admiration and longing. The sight of her, so serene and beautiful against the winter landscape, stirred something deep within him. Determined to bring some clarity and perhaps steer her thoughts back toward their shared future, Joseph decided to ask Emma to accompany him to the upcoming church Christmas pageant.

It was an event that held significance in their community, a time of joy, reflection, and togetherness. He hoped that by sharing this moment with her, he could remind Emma of the strength and beauty of their traditions.

He found her by the edge of the stream, lost in thought. The stream was partially frozen, the ice creating delicate patterns on the surface, while the water continued to flow gently beneath. The trees around them were bare, their branches etched starkly against the pale winter sky. Snow covered the ground, muffling the sounds of their steps as Joseph approached.

"Emma," he called softly, not wanting to startle her.

She looked up, her blue eyes meeting his with a gentle warmth. She was bundled up in a thick woolen coat, her hands encased in knitted gloves, and a soft scarf wrapped around her neck. The sight of her, so close yet so far, made Joseph's heart ache even more. "Joseph, what brings you here?"

"I wanted to ask you something," he began, his voice steady despite the nervous flutter in his chest. "Will you come to the Christmas pageant with me?"

Emma's smile faltered, and Joseph's heart sank. He could see the conflict in her eyes, the struggle she was facing. "Joseph, I... I don't think I can."

"Why not?" he asked, trying to keep the disappointment out of his voice. The stream's gentle babbling seemed to amplify the tension between them.

She hesitated, looking down at her hands, which were clasped tightly together. "I've been praying a lot, asking Gott for guidance. I care about you, Joseph, but my feelings are so confused right now. It feels unfair to you."

Joseph nodded, forcing a smile. The chill in the air seemed to seep into his bones, but he pushed it aside, focusing on Emma. "I understand, Emma. It's all right. Just know that I'm here for you, if you need to talk."

She reached out and squeezed his hand, the contact sending a jolt through him. Her gloved hand felt warm and reassuring. "Thank you, Joseph. That means a lot to me."

He looked around, taking in the frozen stream and the quiet beauty of the winter landscape. The snow-covered banks and the stillness of the woods made it feel like they were in a world apart from everything else, a place where time stood still. "This stream," he said softly, "it brings back memories of playing in the stream with Ruth back in Ohio."

Emma looked at him, her eyes full of empathy. "I wish I would have known Ruth. I'm sure we would have been great friends."

Joseph felt a lump form in his throat as he nodded. "Yes, you would have been. We'd play by the stream for hours, even in the winter. She loved the snow."

He could almost see her now, her bright laughter echoing through the trees, her cheeks flushed with the cold. The memory was both painful and precious. "I miss her every day," he continued, his voice thick with emotion. "Especially around Christmas."

Emma's grip on his hand tightened. "I can't imagine how hard it must be for you, Joseph. Ruth was so special."

He took a deep breath, the cold air stinging his lungs. "She was. Sometimes, I think... if I had been more careful, she might still be here."

"Joseph, it wasn't your fault," Emma said softly. "You were just a boy. It was a tragic accident."

"I know," he replied, his voice barely above a whisper. "It's hard not to blame myself. I was supposed to protect her."

Emma's eyes filled with tears, and she moved closer, her presence a comfort against the cold. "You loved her, Joseph. She knew that."

Joseph looked out at the frozen stream, the memories swirling around him. He remembered the way Ruth's eyes would light up when they played, the way she would tease him and make him laugh. She had been a bright light in his life, and her absence left a void that he didn't know how to fill.

"She was always so brave," he said, his voice trembling. "I... I just want to make her proud."

"You do, Joseph," Emma said firmly. "Every day. By being the kind, caring person you are."

Joseph felt a surge of gratitude and affection for Emma. Her words, her presence, and her understanding meant more to him than she could know. "Thank you, Emma," he said, his voice steadying. "Thank you for being here."

They stood in silence for a moment, the only sounds the gentle flow of the stream and the soft whisper of the wind through the trees. The world around them felt peaceful, almost sacred, as if it were holding its breath along with them.

Joseph turned to Emma, his heart full. "I'll wait, Emma. For as long as it takes. Just know that I care about you, and I'll be here when you're ready."

Emma nodded, her eyes shining with unshed tears. "I've been thinking a lot about us, Joseph. About everything. I want to be fair to you, and to myself. I need to trust in Gott's plan for me, and I hope you can find peace in your heart, too."

Joseph squeezed her hand, drawing strength from her presence. Her words resonated deeply with him, echoing his own prayers for clarity and guidance. "I'll try, Emma. I'll pray for guidance, just like you."

They sat there for a while longer, the weight of their feelings hanging in the air, mingling with the cool evening breeze. The sun dipped below the horizon, casting a warm, golden glow that gradually gave way to the twinkling of the first stars. Joseph felt a sense of calm settle over him, a quiet acceptance that perhaps this Christmas, he could begin to let go of the past and open his heart to the future, whatever it might hold.

The stream beside them continued its gentle flow, a soothing sound that mirrored the slow, steady process of healing within Joseph. Emma's presence, her understanding and compassion, made him believe that he could find a way to honor Ruth's memory without being consumed by guilt and sorrow.

As they walked back toward the farmhouse, the crisp air nipped at their faces, but Joseph hardly felt the cold. He was warmed by the resolve that had taken root in his heart. He would continue to be there for Emma, supporting her in whatever way she needed. He would work on forgiving himself, finding a way to remember Ruth with love and not just pain.

When they reached the farmhouse, the glow from the windows spilled out onto the snow-covered ground, creating a path of light that felt welcoming and hopeful. They stood there for a moment, the silence between them filled with unspoken thoughts and shared understanding.

Joseph turned to Emma, his expression earnest. "Emma, I know I asked earlier, but... would you reconsider coming to the Christmas pageant with me? It's important to me, and I'd love to share it with you."

Emma's face softened, but there was a firmness in her eyes that Joseph hadn't seen before. She took a deep breath, gathering her thoughts. "Joseph, I care about you deeply. You've always been such a good friend to me. But I have to be honest with you—going to the pageant with you right now would give you the wrong impression. My feelings are still so confused."

Joseph's heart sank, but he nodded, trying to hide his disappointment. "I understand, Emma. I really do. I just want what's best for you."

Emma reached out and touched his arm, her touch gentle but decisive. "Thank you, Joseph. I hope you can understand that I need time to sort things out, without any pressure."

He forced a smile, though it didn't reach his eyes. "Of course, Emma. Take all the time you need."

Her eyes filled with gratitude, and she stepped closer, giving him a brief, heartfelt hug. "I appreciate that more than you know, Joseph. You're a wonderful person."

As she pulled away, Joseph felt a profound sense of loss, but also a deep respect for her honesty. He watched as she turned and walked into the farmhouse, her figure illuminated by the warm light from inside. He stood there for a moment longer, the cold seeping into his bones, but his mind was filled with thoughts of Emma and the future he still hoped they could share.

Turning away, he began to make his way back home, his footsteps crunching in the snow. Each step felt heavier than the last, but he knew he had to keep moving forward. He had promised Emma he would pray for guidance, and he intended to keep that promise. His heart ached with disappointment, but he held on to the hope that in time, things might change.

As he walked, he thought about Ruth and the promise he had made to himself to honor her memory. He realized that part of that promise meant accepting the past and finding a way to live fully in the present. He needed to be patient, both with Emma and with himself.

His family's farmhouse came into view, a sturdy structure with a faint glow from the windows indicating his parents were still up. The familiar sight usually brought him comfort, but tonight it felt different. He couldn't shake the feeling of isolation that settled over him as he approached.

Reaching his home, Joseph paused at the door and looked up at the sky. The stars were bright and clear, a reminder of the constancy and beauty of the world around him. He took a deep breath, feeling a sense of peace settle over him.

"Gott," he whispered, "help me to find the strength to be patient, to be understanding, and to trust in your plan for us all."

With that prayer in his heart, Joseph stepped forward, ready to face whatever the future held, with faith, hope, and a steadfast devotion to those he loved.

Opening the door, Joseph was greeted by the warmth of the fireplace and the faint smell of stew lingering in the air. His mother, Martha, was sitting at the kitchen table, her hands busy with mending a piece of clothing. She looked up briefly as he entered but quickly returned to her work. His father, Samuel, sat in his usual chair by the fire, reading a worn Bible, his expression stern and focused.

"Evening, Joseph," his mother said, her tone neutral. "Did you get everything done?"

"Evening, Mamm," Joseph replied, hanging up his coat and scarf. "Yes, I did."

His father looked up, his eyes briefly meeting Joseph's. "Good. There's more work to be done tomorrow. Don't stay up too late."

Joseph nodded, feeling the familiar sting of their distant, almost cold interactions. His parents had never been particularly affectionate, but since Ruth's death, a palpable tension had settled over their home. He couldn't help but feel they blamed him for what had happened, even if they never said it outright.

Martha's hands never stopped moving, the needle and thread weaving in and out of the fabric with practiced ease. "Supper's on the stove if you're hungry," she said, not looking up.

"Thank you, Mamm," Joseph said quietly. He served himself a bowl of the stew and sat at the table, the warmth of the food doing little to ease the chill in his heart.

The silence in the room was heavy, broken only by the crackling of the fire and the occasional turn of a page from his father's Bible. Joseph ate slowly, his thoughts drifting back to Emma and their conversation by the stream. He longed for the warmth and understanding he found in her company, a contrast to the cold, distant atmosphere of his home.

After finishing his meal, Joseph washed his bowl and set it on the drying rack. He glanced at his parents, who were still engrossed in their tasks, and felt a pang of longing for the closeness they once shared.

Ruth's absence had created a void that none of them seemed able to fill.

"I'm going to bed," he said softly, more out of habit than expectation of a response.

"Goodnight, Joseph," his mother replied, her voice devoid of warmth.

"Goodnight," his father echoed, not looking up from his reading.

Joseph climbed the stairs to his room, each step feeling heavier than the last. He closed the door behind him and sat on the edge of his bed, the weight of the day pressing down on him. He pulled out the small wooden box from under his bed, where he kept Ruth's favorite ribbon. Holding it in his hands, he felt the familiar ache of loss.

As he lay down, Joseph prayed for strength and guidance. "Gott, help me to find peace. Help me to honor Ruth's memory and to be patient with Emma. Show me the path you have for me."

With that prayer in his heart, Joseph closed his eyes, the hope of a new day mingling with the pain of the past. He knew the journey ahead would not be easy, but he was determined to face it with faith and resolve.

Chapter Four

The next evening, Emma walked downstairs, her mind still buzzing with the previous evening's events. Her parents were in the kitchen, finishing up the last of the dinner preparations. The warm glow of the oil lamps and the comforting aroma of stew filled the air, but Emma's thoughts were elsewhere. Maria looked up as Emma entered, her brow furrowing slightly in concern.

"Everything all right, Emma?" her mother asked, pausing in her work.

"Yes, Mamm," Emma replied, offering a reassuring smile she didn't feel. "Joseph and I just had a talk yesterday, and it's been on my mind."

Maria's expression softened, misunderstanding. "I'm glad to hear that. Joseph is a good man."

Emma nodded, the weight of her decision settling in her chest like a stone. "Yes, he is."

As she helped her mother set the table, laying out the simple yet elegant dishes and arranging the bread and butter, Emma's mind wandered to the Christmas pageant. It had always been one of her favorite events, filled with music, joy, and the warmth of the community coming together.

"Emma, can you bring the stew to the table?" Maria's voice broke through her thoughts.

"Of course, Mamm," Emma replied, lifting the heavy pot and carefully carrying it to the table. As she served her father and mother, she couldn't help but think about the conversation she had with Joseph by the stream. His sincerity, his pain, and his unwavering support had touched her deeply. She wished she could find the clarity she so desperately sought.

After dinner, Emma helped with the dishes, her hands moving automatically through the familiar motions. Her father, Abram, talked about the day's work and plans for the farm, but Emma found it hard to focus. Her thoughts kept drifting back to Joseph and the Christmas pageant.

When the chores were done and the kitchen was finally clean, Emma bid her parents goodnight and climbed the stairs to her room. The moonlight filtered through the window, casting a soft glow on the simple furniture. She knelt by her bed, folding her hands in prayer.

"Dear Gott," she whispered, "please guide me. Help me to see the right path and to open my heart to what is true and good. Amen."

As she climbed into bed, Emma felt a sense of calm wash over her. She didn't know what the future held, but she was willing to trust in Gott's plan. She pulled the warm quilt up to her chin and let out a deep sigh, the events of the day playing over in her mind. The memory of Joseph's earnest eyes and his gentle words filled her with a tentative hope.

Maybe, just maybe, that plan included finding love and happiness with Joseph.

***

The next morning, Emma woke to the soft light of dawn filtering through her window. She stretched, feeling the weight of the previous day's decisions still pressing on her. With a sigh, she rose and dressed in her usual plain blue dress and apron, carefully tying her prayer kapp in place.

Downstairs, the house was still quiet. Emma moved silently, starting the stove and preparing breakfast for her daed. She mixed the batter for pancakes, adding a bit of cinnamon just the way he liked, and set the table with simple, sturdy dishes.

As the pancakes cooked, she gathered fresh eggs from the basket on the counter and fried them in the skillet. The familiar sizzle and the scent of cooking food brought a sense of normalcy, grounding her in the routine of daily life. Despite her swirling thoughts, these small tasks provided a comforting rhythm.

Her daed entered the kitchen, his face lighting up at the sight of the breakfast spread. "Good morning, Emma," he greeted, his voice warm.

"Good morning, Daed," she replied, offering him a plate. "Breakfast is ready."

Abram sat down, his expression content as he began to eat. "Thank you, Emma. This is wonderful."

She smiled, watching him for a moment before turning back to the stove to prepare her own plate. They ate in companionable silence; the only sounds the clink of cutlery and the occasional murmur of appreciation from her daed.

After breakfast, Abram stood, ready to head out to work on the farm. "I've got to tend to the fields today," he said. "Thank you for the meal."

"You're welcome, Daed," Emma replied, clearing the table. "I'll take care of the dishes."

As Abram left the kitchen, Emma felt a pang of anxiety. She knew Ross would be arriving soon to tend to the horses, but she couldn't face him. The thought of his knowing eyes and gentle demeanor made her heart race with a mix of embarrassment and uncertainty. How could she look at him when she knew she had hurt Joseph so?

She busied herself with the dishes, trying to push the thoughts away, but they lingered. The sound of Ross's truck arriving made her tense. She heard him talking to her daed outside, his deep voice carrying through the open window.

Emma took a deep breath, focusing on her tasks. She washed the dishes meticulously, dried them, and put them away. She swept the kitchen floor, wiped down the counters, and even rearranged the jars of preserves in the pantry, anything to keep herself occupied and away from Ross.

Her mother was outside doing the washing, the rhythmic motion of her arms as she scrubbed and wrung out the clothes almost hypnotic. Emma glanced out the window, seeing Ross approach the barn. Her heart ached with a confusing mix of emotions.

What did that mean for her future? Could she really open her heart to Joseph and leave her feelings for Ross behind?

The morning passed in a blur of chores and introspection. Emma tried to keep busy, but her thoughts kept circling back to the two men who occupied her heart in such different ways. By midday, she was exhausted, both physically and emotionally.

As she finished folding the last of the clean laundry, her mother came inside, wiping her hands on her apron. "Emma, are you all right?" Maria asked, her voice gentle with concern.

Emma looked up, forcing a small smile. "I'm fine, Mamm. Just a lot on my mind."

Maria's eyes softened with understanding. "You've been through a lot lately. It's okay to feel overwhelmed."

Emma set down the folded towel and sighed. "I know, Mamm. It's just...everything feels so complicated."

Maria walked over and placed a comforting hand on Emma's shoulder. "Tell me what's on your mind, dear."

Emma hesitated, then took a deep breath. "I'm thinking about going to the pageant with Joseph. I don't want to lead him on, but I feel like I owe him a chance. I haven't told him yet."

Maria nodded slowly, her expression thoughtful. "Emma, it's natural to feel conflicted. You need to consider what's best for your future. Joseph is a good man, and he understands our ways."

Emma looked down, her voice barely above a whisper. "What if I never feel for Joseph what I feel for Ross?"

Her mother's face tightened slightly, a hint of impatience creeping into her eyes. "Emma, feelings can grow. You can learn to love Joseph. Sometimes, the heart follows where the mind leads. You need to give it time."

Emma felt a flicker of frustration. "Mamm, it's not that simple. My feelings for Ross are strong, even if I know they can't go anywhere. It's hard to just ignore that."

Maria's tone sharpened, her patience wearing thin. "Emma, you can't spend your life chasing after something that isn't meant to be. Ross is an Englischer. That life is not for you. You need to focus on what's right in front of you, and that's Joseph. He's here, he cares for you, and he's willing to build a life with you."

Emma's eyes filled with tears. "What if I never feel the same way about him? What if I can't?"

Maria took a deep breath, trying to calm herself. "Emma, you're young. You need to trust that love can grow from friendship. You're letting your emotions cloud your judgment."

Emma's frustration boiled over. "Mamm, you don't understand! I can't just force myself to feel something that isn't there."

Maria's patience snapped. "Emma, you're being foolish! You're so focused on what you think you want that you're ignoring what's best for you. Don't make a mess of things because you're too stubborn to see what you really need."

Emma felt a sharp sting of hurt and anger. "You're not listening to me! You're just trying to push me into something I'm not ready for."

Maria's eyes flashed with anger and worry. "I'm trying to protect you, Emma. I don't want to see you throw away your future for a fantasy."

Emma couldn't hold back the tears any longer. "Maybe I need to figure things out on my own," she said, her voice breaking.

Maria's expression softened slightly, but the frustration was still there. "Fine, Emma. Don't forget, you're not just making decisions for yourself. Your choices affect all of us."

Unable to take any more, Emma turned and fled to her room, the tears streaming down her face. She closed the door behind her and sank onto her bed, burying her face in her hands. The argument with her mother echoed in her mind, leaving her feeling more confused and upset than ever.

She knew her mother was only trying to help, but the pressure to make the right choice felt overwhelming. She needed clarity, but it seemed further away than ever. As she lay there, the weight of her emotions pressing down on her, Emma prayed for guidance, hoping that somehow, she would find the strength to navigate the path ahead.

Chapter Five

As the days slipped by and the Christmas pageant approached, Emma noticed that Joseph had been avoiding her since she refused to attend the event with him. It was subtle, but she sensed it in the way he kept his distance and the way his eyes no longer sought hers as often. This change in their dynamic left her feeling uneasy and more than a little guilty. She had always valued Joseph's friendship and his unwavering support, but now it felt as though a wall had been erected between them, one she wasn't sure how to tear down.

One afternoon, Emma decided to visit the community center to see how the preparations were coming along. The building was a hub of activity, with children and adults alike bustling about, setting up decorations and rehearsing their lines.

As she stepped inside, the sound of Joseph's voice, clear and strong, echoed through the hall. He was guiding a small group of children through their lines, his patience seemingly endless. Emma watched from a distance, her heart twisting with a mix of admiration and uncertainty.

It was then that she noticed her friend Catherine standing nearby, talking with Joseph. Catherine's eyes sparkled with laughter, and Joseph appeared to be enjoying their conversation a little too much for Emma's liking. She felt a sharp pang of something unfamiliar—jealousy. It was a new and uncomfortable feeling, one that made her chest tighten and her steps falter.

Emma had never felt this way about Joseph before. He had always been a friend, someone steady and dependable. Now, seeing him with Catherine, Emma felt a strange possessiveness rise within her. It was as if she was seeing him in a new light, and she wasn't sure what to make of it.

Catherine turned and saw Emma, her face lighting up. "Emma! Come join us!" she called, waving her over.

Forcing a smile, Emma walked over to them. "Hello, Catherine. Joseph," she greeted, trying to keep her voice steady and her jealousy hidden.

"Hi, Emma," Joseph said, his smile warm but cautious, as if he was unsure of how to act around her now.

Catherine beamed, her enthusiasm undimmed. "Joseph has been such a great help with the children. They adore him."

Emma nodded, her eyes flicking between the two of them. "Yes, he's always been good with kids."

As they chatted, Emma felt a growing discomfort. She couldn't shake the jealousy gnawing at her, especially when Catherine seemed to lean a little too close to Joseph, her laughter a little too bright. The sight of them together, so at ease in each other's company, only heightened Emma's sense of unease.

Finally, unable to take it any longer, Emma excused herself and stepped outside to catch her breath. The cold winter air hit her face, a stark contrast to the warmth inside, but it did little to cool the turmoil in her heart. She leaned against the wall of the community center, trying to steady her breathing and calm her racing thoughts.

Why did it bother her so much to see Joseph with Catherine? She had always thought of him as a friend, nothing more. Now, seeing him laugh and smile with someone else, she realized that her feelings might be deeper than she had admitted to herself.

The realization was both startling and confusing. She had been so focused on her conflicting feelings for Ross and her responsibilities to her family and community that she hadn't considered the possibility that she might have feelings for Joseph, too. The jealousy she felt watching him with Catherine was a clear sign that her heart was more entangled than she had realized.

Emma stood there, her mind swirling with thoughts and emotions. The sounds of laughter and chatter from inside the community center drifted out to her, reminding her of the world she was momentarily hiding from. She knew she couldn't stay out there forever. She had to face Joseph, and perhaps, her own feelings.

As she considered going back inside, the door opened, and Catherine stepped out. Emma's heart sank as she saw her friend approaching, her face glowing with the same cheerfulness that had so unnerved her moments before. Catherine didn't seem to notice Emma's discomfort as she walked over, a bright smile on her face.

Emma took a deep breath, steeling herself for the conversation she knew was coming.

"Emma, is everything all right?"

Emma forced another smile, though it felt brittle. "Yes, I'm fine. Just needed some air."

Catherine hesitated, then spoke in a softer tone. "Emma, can I tell you something?"

"Of course," Emma replied, trying to mask the unease she felt.

Catherine glanced around, ensuring no one else was within earshot, then leaned in slightly. "I've always thought Joseph was a good man. He's just so kind and good with the children. I thought maybe...I don't know, that there might be a chance for us."

Emma's heart clenched at Catherine's confession. The jealousy flared brighter, mingling with guilt. She felt a knot tightening in her chest. "I didn't know," she said quietly, struggling to keep her emotions in check.

Catherine sighed, her expression conflicted. "I know you and Joseph have a history, and I don't want to come between you two. I just thought you should know how I feel."

Emma nodded, her mind racing. "Thank you for telling me, Catherine. I appreciate your honesty."

Catherine gave her a small, understanding smile. "I hope this doesn't change anything between us, Emma. I value our friendship too much to let anything come between us."

"Me too," Emma managed, though her voice was barely above a whisper.

As Catherine returned to the community center, Emma stayed outside, her thoughts a whirlwind of confusion. The jealousy she felt was undeniable, and it forced her to confront feelings she hadn't fully acknowledged before. Maybe there was more to her relationship with Joseph than she had been willing to see.

Emma lingered outside the community center, the cold air nipping at her cheeks as she tried to sort through the jumble of emotions swirling within her. She had always seen Joseph as a steady, reliable friend, someone she could count on. Now, seeing him through Catherine's eyes, she realized there might be deeper feelings hidden beneath the surface.

After a few moments of composing herself, she decided to head back inside to try and speak to Joseph. Maybe she could clear the air, and perhaps even sort out her own feelings in the process.

As she stepped back into the warm, bustling hall, she saw people beginning to pack up. The children were being gathered by their parents, and the decorations were being carefully stored away for the next rehearsal. Emma scanned the room, her eyes searching for Joseph.

She spotted him near the back, but her heart sank when she saw that Catherine was already with him. They were standing close, talking and laughing as they put away costumes and props. Joseph's warm smile and the way he seemed so at ease with Catherine made the pang of jealousy sharper now than before. Emma felt a sinking feeling in her stomach as she watched them, a painful reminder of the unresolved feelings she was grappling with.

She took a step forward, intending to approach them, but hesitated. Her resolve wavered as she saw the genuine connection between Joseph and Catherine. Doubts flooded her mind. What if she misinterpreted her feelings? What if she wasn't ready to face the truth about her heart?

The room felt suddenly claustrophobic, the cheerful chatter and laughter of the other volunteers ringing hollow in her ears. Emma's breath quickened as she struggled with the decision of whether to speak to Joseph or retreat. The fear of complicating things, of adding more confusion to an already tangled situation, made her hesitate.

Finally, Emma decided not to talk to him. She couldn't bear to interrupt the moment between Joseph and Catherine, and the thought of exposing her own uncertainties felt too overwhelming. She turned away, her steps heavy with indecision.

Before she could dart out of sight, however, Joseph caught her gaze from across the room.

Joseph looked up then, his expression unreadable. "Hello, Emma," he called out, his voice neutral.

"Hi, Joseph," she replied, involuntarily walking towards him, trying to keep her tone light. There was no avoiding him now; it was better to act calm. "I just wanted to see if you needed any help."

"We're almost done here," he said, glancing back at Catherine. "Thanks, though."

Emma's heart sank further. She could feel the distance between them, and it hurt more than she expected. She stood there awkwardly for a moment, unsure of what to do next.

Then, Catherine spoke up. "Joseph, would you mind giving me a ride home? My daed took our buggy to town, and I'd rather not walk in this cold."

Joseph nodded, turning to her with a smile. "Of course, Catherine. Let's get going then."

Emma watched as they gathered their things and headed out to the buggy. Her chest tightened as she saw Joseph help Catherine into the seat, his hand lingering just a moment longer than necessary. She felt a surge of emotions—jealousy, confusion, and a strange new awareness of her feelings for him.

As the buggy pulled away, Emma stood frozen in place. The sight of Joseph and Catherine together, so comfortable and happy, made her realize that she might have stronger feelings for him than she had ever admitted to herself. The idea of losing him to someone else, especially someone as close as Catherine, was almost unbearable.

She turned back towards the community center, where people were finishing tidying up and putting away the decorations. The children's laughter echoed faintly, blending with the muffled conversations of the adults as they prepared to leave. Emma's footsteps were slow and heavy as she made her way through the bustling hall, her eyes scanning for something to keep her occupied.

"Emma!" called Mrs. Lapp, waving her over from a corner where she was packing up craft supplies. "Could you give me a hand with these decorations?"

"Of course," Emma replied, grateful for the distraction. She joined Mrs. Lapp, carefully wrapping fragile ornaments in tissue paper and placing them into a box.

"I saw you talking with Joseph and Catherine," Mrs. Lapp remarked casually. "Those two make quite a team, don't they?"

Emma forced a smile. "Yes, they do."

As they worked together, Emma's mind kept drifting back to Joseph and Catherine. She tried to focus on the task at hand, but her thoughts were a constant undercurrent of uncertainty and longing.

The room gradually emptied as families collected their children and made their way home. Emma glanced around, feeling the growing emptiness of the hall. She handed the last box of decorations to Mrs. Lapp, who thanked her warmly.

"You should head home, dear," Mrs. Lapp said, patting her arm. "It's getting late, and the roads will be icy."

Emma nodded, putting on her coat. "Thank you, Mrs. Lapp. Have a good night."

"You too, Emma. And take care," Mrs. Lapp replied with a knowing look.

Emma stepped outside, the cold air biting at her cheeks. The sky was darkening, the first stars beginning to twinkle above. She took a deep breath, trying to steady her nerves, then started the walk home. The crunch of the snow beneath her boots was the only sound in the stillness of the evening.

The moon cast a pale glow on the landscape, turning the familiar path home into a scene from a dream. The trees stood like silent sentinels, their branches heavy with snow. Emma's breath formed small clouds in the frigid air as she walked, her steps slow and deliberate.

She passed the fields, now blanketed in snow, their usual boundaries softened by the white cover. The farmhouse came into view, its windows glowing warmly against the cold night. Emma hesitated for a moment at the gate, looking up at the sky. She whispered a silent prayer for guidance before making her way to the front door.

Inside, the familiar scents of supper cooking and the sounds of her parents talking softly brought a small measure of comfort. She hung her coat by the door and walked into the kitchen, where her mother was stirring a pot on the stove.

"Everything all right, Emma?" Maria asked, looking up with a gentle smile.

"Yes, Mamm," Emma replied, returning the smile as best she could. "Just tired."

Abram looked up from his seat at the table, his face concerned. "You look troubled. Is something on your mind?"

Emma shook her head, trying to dismiss the swirling emotions. "Just a lot to think about."

Maria and Abram exchanged a glance, but neither pressed her further. They sat down to dinner, the warmth of the meal and the familiarity of family providing some solace. Emma picked at her food, her thoughts drifting back to the community center, to Joseph and Catherine.

After dinner, Emma helped her mother with the dishes, the simple chore grounding her in the present. The clinking of plates and the running water were soothing, a rhythm that contrasted with the chaos in her heart.

When the kitchen was clean, Emma excused herself and climbed the stairs to her room. The moonlight filtered through the window, casting a soft glow on the simple furniture. She knelt by her bed, folding her hands in prayer.

"Dear Gott," she whispered, "please guide me. Help me to see the right path and to open my heart to what is true and good. Amen."

As she climbed into bed, Emma felt a sense of calm wash over her. She didn't know what the future held, but she was willing to trust in Gott's plan. She pulled the warm quilt up to her chin and let out a deep sigh, the events of the day playing over in her mind. The memory of Joseph's earnest eyes and his gentle words filled her with a tentative hope. Maybe, just maybe, that plan included finding love and happiness with Joseph.

Chapter Six

The next day, Emma rose early to help her father with the farm work. The winter air was crisp, and the morning sky was a pale blue, promising a clear day. She dressed quickly, her mind still tangled with thoughts of Joseph and the confusing emotions that had surfaced.

Downstairs, she found her father already preparing for the day. Abram greeted her with a warm smile. "Morning, Emma. Ready to tackle the chores?"

"Good morning, Daed," she replied, trying to match his enthusiasm. "Yes, I'm ready."

They headed out to the barn together, the ground crunching under their boots. The familiar routine of feeding the animals and checking the fences provided a welcome distraction from her swirling thoughts. As they worked, Emma found herself glancing toward the paddock where the horses were kept. She knew Ross would be arriving soon to check on them.

Sure enough, as they finished up with the cows, Emma saw Ross's truck pull up. He stepped out, carrying his veterinary bag, and headed toward the barn. Emma's heart skipped a beat, a mix of excitement and anxiety flooding her senses. Her mother, Maria, was already there, waiting for Ross to examine the horses, who were feeling much better after having been ill.

"Good morning, Ross," Maria greeted him warmly. "Thank you for coming by."

"My pleasure, Maria," Ross replied with a smile. "How are the horses doing today?"

"They seem much improved, thanks to your care," Maria said, leading him to the paddock.

Emma watched from a distance, feeling a pang of something she couldn't quite identify. As Ross tended to the horses, speaking softly to them and moving with a practiced ease, Emma's thoughts drifted back to Joseph. She remembered how she had felt seeing him with Catherine, the jealousy that had flared up unexpectedly. The intensity of it surprised her; she had always thought of

Joseph as a friend, but now, things seemed more complicated.

Ross moved with confidence, his hands gentle yet firm as he examined the horses. He spoke softly to them, his voice calming and reassuring. Emma admired his skill and dedication, qualities that had always drawn her to him. Today, there was a heaviness in her heart that made it difficult to fully appreciate his presence.

Maria and Ross discussed the horses' recovery, their voices a low murmur against the backdrop of the farm. Emma busied herself with her tasks, trying to focus on the familiar routines that had always brought her comfort. She cleaned out the stalls, the rhythmic motions providing a temporary escape from her tangled thoughts.

"Emma, could you bring some fresh hay?" Abram called from the other side of the barn.

"Yes, Daed," she replied, grateful for the distraction. She lifted a bale of hay, carrying it over to where her father was working. The physical effort helped to clear her mind, if only for a moment.

As she spread the hay in the stalls, she couldn't help but overhear snippets of Ross's conversation with her mother.

"These new medications should help maintain their health," Ross was saying. "It's important to follow the dosage instructions carefully."

Maria nodded, her expression serious. "We'll make sure to do that, Ross. Thank you for everything."

"It's my job," Ross replied with a modest smile. "I'm glad to see they're improving."

Emma paused in her work, watching Ross as he explained the treatment plan to her mother. His dedication and care for the animals were evident in every word he spoke. She felt a warmth in her chest, a reminder of why she had been drawn to him in the first place.

As she turned back to her work, spreading the hay with deliberate movements, her thoughts once again drifted to Joseph. The memory of his expression when she had refused to go to the pageant with him haunted her. The distance that had grown between them, the sight of him with Catherine—all of it weighed heavily on her heart.

Emma finished her task and leaned against the barn wall for a moment, closing her eyes. The cool air was refreshing, a stark contrast to the turmoil within her. She knew she needed to sort out her feelings, to find a way to reconcile her emotions and make a decision that would bring her peace.

As Ross and Maria continued their discussion, Emma listened, but her mind was only half on their words. She was grateful for the presence of the people she cared about, but the confusion in her heart made it hard to fully engage.

"Emma," Ross called, his voice breaking through her reverie. "Could you come here for a moment?"

Emma straightened, pushing her thoughts aside as she walked over to where Ross and her mother stood. "Yes, Ross?"

"I just wanted to show you how to administer the medication," Ross said, holding out a small bottle. "It's important that you know what to do in case I'm not around."

Emma nodded, taking the bottle from him and listening carefully as he explained the process. She appreciated his thoroughness, his desire to ensure the horses received the best care possible.

"Thank you, Ross," she said, once he had finished. "I'll make sure to follow your instructions."

Ross smiled, his eyes warm. "I know you will, Emma. You're very capable."

His words brought a small measure of comfort, a reminder that she was valued and trusted.

Still, speaking with Ross didn't bring the same warmth it once had, the same flushed cheeks and fast heartbeat. She realized, then, why that was.

Decision made, she said, "Mamm, I think I'll head into town and visit the community center again."

Maria looked up, surprised. "So soon, Emma? You've been working hard all morning."

Emma nodded, trying to appear nonchalant. "I just need to check on a few things and see if they need any help."

Abram smiled warmly. "All right, Emma. Be careful. The weather looks like it might change."

"I will, Daed," Emma assured him, already grabbing her coat from on top of the haystack where she had put it earlier.

As she stepped outside, the winter air bit at her cheeks, but she barely felt it, her mind focused on what she needed to do. She walked quickly, her heart racing as she made her way to the community center. The familiar path was covered in a fresh layer of snow, the world around her silent except for the crunch of her boots on the ground.

When she arrived at the community center, it was quieter than usual. Most people were likely busy with their own preparations for the holiday. She entered the building, her footsteps echoing in the empty halls. Her anxiety grew with each empty space she encountered, her mind racing with thoughts of what she needed to say to Joseph.

Finally, she found him in the small storeroom at the back, sorting through decorations. The room was dimly lit, the faint glow of a single bulb casting long shadows on the walls. Joseph looked up as she entered, a mixture of surprise and something else—relief?—in his eyes.

"Emma," he said, setting down the box he was holding. "What are you doing here?"

She took a deep breath, her nerves threatening to overwhelm her. "Joseph, I need to talk to you."

He nodded, his expression serious. "Of course. What is it?"

Emma opened her mouth to speak, to tell him how she had come to realize her true feelings and that she wanted to go to the pageant with him, but before she could get the words out, Mrs. Lapp, one of the older women from the community, poked her head into the room.

"Joseph, Emma, I'm sorry to interrupt, but we could use some help with the decorations in the main hall. It seems there's been a mix-up, and we need to rearrange a few things," Mrs. Lapp said, her voice kind but urgent.

Emma glanced at Joseph, feeling the weight of the moment slipping away. She wanted to tell him now, but the urgency in Mrs. Lapp's voice made her hesitate.

"Of course, Mrs. Lapp. We'll be right there," Joseph replied, looking back at Emma with a hint of regret in his eyes.

Emma nodded, forcing a smile. "We'll talk later," she said softly.

Joseph gave her a reassuring nod before they followed Mrs. Lapp out of the storeroom. The main hall was bustling with activity, and the need for assistance was apparent. Emma tried to focus on the task at hand, but her mind kept drifting back to what she needed to say to Joseph.

As they worked, the atmosphere in the community center grew tense. The snow started falling outside but then changed to rain, a reminder that a storm was approaching. Emma's heart pounded, the urgency of her feelings pressing against the demands of the moment.

Just as she was about to turn to Joseph and try to speak to him again, the sound of rain had her thoughts turning to leaving and trying to get home. The lanterns flickered briefly, casting a momentary shadow over the room.

"We'd better hurry," Mrs. Lapp said, her voice tinged with concern. "This storm looks like it's going to be a big one."

Emma nodded, her resolve wavering as she glanced at Joseph. She knew she needed to tell him how she felt, but the timing seemed impossible. With the storm approaching, there was little they could do but focus on the immediate tasks at hand.

As they worked side by side, Emma felt a mix of frustration and determination. She had come this far, and she wasn't going to let a storm stand in the way of what she needed to say. She just hoped that when the time finally came, she would find the courage to speak her heart.

"Joseph, Emma, you two should be heading home soon," Mrs. Lapp said as they fixed the last decoration, her voice tinged with urgency. "The snow and rain have stopped, for now at least."

Emma frowned, glancing out the window. The sky had been clear when she arrived. But she knew how clear skies could turn to rain, snow or sleet in a matter of minutes.

Mrs. Lapp nodded gravely. "Oh dear, the rain is falling again. Off you go you two; it's best not to get caught in a storm."

Joseph moved to the window, peering outside. His eyes widened slightly at the sight of dark clouds gathering on the horizon. "She's right, Emma. We should get going."

Emma felt a surge of frustration. She had finally worked up the courage to talk to Joseph, and now this. She glanced outside again, noting the ominous sky. "I just got here. We were in the middle of something important."

Joseph looked at her with a mix of concern and regret. "We can talk later, Emma. Right now, we need to make sure everyone gets home safely."

Emma bit back her annoyance, knowing he was right but feeling thwarted nonetheless. She watched as Joseph went to speak with some of the other men, coordinating the efforts to ensure everyone left quickly and safely. Her chance to speak to him had slipped away again, and she felt a knot of anxiety and disappointment tighten in her chest.

As people hurried to gather their things and head home, Emma lingered, hoping for a brief moment alone with Joseph. He was busy, his attention fully occupied with the logistics of getting everyone out before the storm hit. Her frustration grew as she realized she wouldn't get the chance to talk to him after all.

With a sigh, Emma put on her coat and stepped outside. The first drops of rain were beginning to fall, and the wind was picking up, sending a chill through the air. She glanced back at the community center, seeing Joseph still engaged in conversation with some of the men. He didn't look her way.

Feeling a mix of disappointment and concern, Emma began her walk home. The rain started to come down harder, soaking through her coat and dress. She quickened her pace, cold and shivering.

As she walked, her thoughts churned. She wondered if the storm would affect the Christmas preparations and if she would get another chance to talk to Joseph before the pageant. The frustration of the missed opportunity gnawed at her. She had been so close to finally telling him how she felt, and now she wasn't sure when she would get another chance.

By the time she reached the farmhouse, she was drenched and shivering. Maria met her at the door, her eyes widening in concern. "Emma, you're soaked! Come inside and get dry."

Emma nodded, stepping into the warmth of the house. "The rain came in so fast, Mamm. We had to leave the community center early."

Maria helped her out of her wet coat and dress, wrapping her in a warm towel. "I see that. Let's hope it passes quickly and doesn't cause too much trouble."

"I hope so, Mamm. If this turns to snow, we'll be snowed in for days."

Emma sat by the fire, drying off and warming up, her thoughts still lingering on Joseph. She hoped the storm wouldn't ruin the Christmas pageant, and more importantly, she hoped she would get another chance to speak with him. The missed opportunity weighed heavily on her, but she knew she had to be patient and wait for the right moment.

As she watched the fire flicker, the storm raging outside, Emma prayed for guidance and strength. She knew she needed to find a way to navigate her feelings and the uncertainties that lay ahead. For now, all she could do was wait and hope for better weather and clearer skies, both outside and within her heart.

Chapter Seven

The weather remained harsh all week, with icy winds and heavy snowfall making the days feel bleak and endless. Emma tried to keep herself busy with chores and preparations for Christmas, but the constant gray skies and the howling wind outside only served to deepen her anxiety. She hadn't had another chance to speak with Joseph since the storm interrupted their conversation, and it weighed heavily on her mind.

A week before Christmas, the community was hit by a severe snowstorm. The wind howled fiercely, and the snow fell in blinding sheets, covering everything in a thick, white blanket. The storm caused damage and panic throughout the community, with roofs collapsing under the weight of the snow and livestock getting lost in the chaos.

The Fisher farm was not spared. In the middle of the night, two of their horses managed to get out of the barn and went missing. Abram Fisher was devastated. The horses were not just valuable assets but also part of the family. Without them, the farm's operations would suffer greatly.

Emma's heart ached seeing her father so distraught. She knew they had to find the horses, and fast. Joseph, ever the dependable neighbor, arrived at their doorstep early the next morning, bundled up against the cold and ready to help.

"Mr. Fisher, Emma," Joseph said, his breath visible in the frosty air, "I heard about the horses. I'll go and find them."

"Thank you, Joseph," Abram said, his voice heavy with worry. "I don't know what we would do without them."

Emma stepped forward, determination in her eyes. "I'm coming with you."

Joseph hesitated, concern etched on his face. "Emma, the weather is terrible. It's going to be dangerous out there."

"I don't care," she replied firmly. "Those horses are part of our family. I need to help find them."

Seeing the resolve in her eyes, Joseph nodded. "All right, let's go then. We need to be careful."

They bundled up in their warmest clothes, scarves wrapped tightly around their faces, and headed out into the biting cold. The snow was deep, and the wind whipped around them, making it difficult to see more than a few feet ahead. They called out for the horses, their voices swallowed by the storm.

They trudged through the snow, their determination keeping them going despite the numbing cold and the howling wind. The snowstorm had descended upon them with a ferocity they hadn't anticipated, and now, visibility was almost zero.

Emma's thoughts were a mix of worry for the lost horses and the tension between her and Joseph. The relentless storm made it impossible to have a proper conversation, and she was desperate to find the right moment to talk to him, to tell him how she felt.

The cold was seeping through their thick coats, their faces numb from the biting wind. They called out for the horses, their voices swallowed by the howling gale. Emma could barely see Joseph, just a few steps ahead of her, his form a shadowy figure against the white landscape. Her heart pounded with anxiety, the fear of being lost in the storm adding to her distress.

"Joseph, do you think we'll find them?" Emma shouted, her voice nearly drowned out by the wind.

Joseph turned back, his face set with determination. "We have to keep trying, Emma. They can't have gone far."

Emma nodded, though she wasn't sure he could see her. She tightened her scarf around her face, trying to shield herself from the cold. Her fingers were numb, and each step felt heavier than the last. The snow was deep, making progress slow and exhausting.

An hour later, they stumbled upon an abandoned barn. The structure was old and weathered, its wooden beams creaking under the weight of the snow. It offered a bleak but welcome sight, a potential respite from the relentless storm.

"We should take shelter here for a while," Joseph said, his voice barely audible over the wind. "It's too dangerous to keep searching in this weather."

Emma nodded, exhausted and grateful for the suggestion. They pushed open the creaky barn door and stepped inside. The interior was dim and cold, but at least it provided a break from the biting wind. The barn was empty except for a few old, rusted farming tools and some straw scattered on the ground. They found a small corner where they could sit and try to warm up.

Emma sank to the floor, pulling her knees to her chest and wrapping her arms around them. She shivered uncontrollably, the cold penetrating every layer of clothing. Joseph sat beside her, close enough that she could feel his body heat.

"Here," Joseph said, taking off his coat and draping it over her shoulders. "You need to stay warm."

Emma protested, "You'll freeze, Joseph."

"I'll be all right," he replied, his tone firm. "You need it more than I do."

She couldn't argue with the kindness in his eyes, so she pulled the coat tighter around herself, grateful for the added warmth. They huddled together, their breaths visible in the frigid air. The wind howled outside, rattling the barn's old wooden walls and creating an eerie symphony of creaks and groans.

Emma's heart raced, not just from the adrenaline but from the proximity to Joseph and the unresolved feelings between them. The fear of the storm and the uncertainty of their situation heightened her emotions, making her acutely aware of every movement, every breath they shared.

"Joseph," she began, her voice trembling. "I... I need to tell you something."

He looked at her, his eyes filled with concern and something else she couldn't quite identify. "What is it, Emma?"

Before she could find the words, a particularly fierce gust of wind shook the barn, causing them both to instinctively huddle closer together. Emma could feel the warmth of Joseph's body through their layers of clothing, and it provided a small but significant comfort.

"Emma, whatever it is, you can tell me," Joseph said softly, his voice steady despite the storm raging outside.

She took a deep breath, trying to steady her nerves. "Joseph, I've been thinking a lot about us, about everything. I realize now that I have feelings for you, stronger than I ever admitted to myself."

Joseph's eyes widened slightly, a mixture of surprise and relief washing over his face. "Emma, I've always cared about you, but is now the time?"

A loud crack interrupted their moment as a piece of the barn's roof gave way under the weight of the snow, sending a flurry of icy particles down on them. Emma gasped, instinctively pressing closer to Joseph for protection.

"We need to find a safer spot," Joseph said urgently, helping her to her feet. They moved to a more stable corner of the barn, the fear of the structure collapsing adding to their already heightened anxiety.

As they settled into their new spot, Emma couldn't help but shiver, both from the cold and the adrenaline coursing through her veins. Joseph wrapped his arm around her, trying to provide as much warmth and comfort as he could.

"We'll get through this, Emma," Joseph whispered, his breath warm against her ear. "I promise."

Emma nodded, feeling a strange sense of peace amidst the chaos. Despite the storm, despite the fear, she felt a deep connection to Joseph, a bond that had been strengthened by their shared ordeal.

As they huddled together for warmth, the reality of their situation settled over them. They were alone, forced to rely on each other in the midst of a raging storm. Emma knew that whatever happened, they would face it together, and that gave her the strength to endure the cold and the fear.

They lapsed into silence for a long time, broken only by the howl of the wind.

After a long moment, Joseph took a deep breath and broke the silence. "Emma, there's something I've been meaning to tell you. Something I haven't shared with many people."

Emma turned to him, her eyes full of concern. "What is it, Joseph?"

He looked down at his hands, his fingers nervously tracing patterns in the dust on the floor. "It's about my sister, Ruth. I told you that she died when we were living in Ohio, but I never told you the whole story."

Emma's heart ached at the mention of Ruth. She remembered overhearing Joseph's parents speaking about the tragedy and saw first-hand how it had affected Joseph's family, but she had never heard the details. She reached out and placed a comforting hand on his arm. "You can tell me, Joseph. I'm here."

Joseph took another deep breath, his voice trembling slightly as he spoke. "It was Christmas Eve. Ruth was so excited about the holiday. She loved the snow, loved playing outside. I was supposed to be watching her, but I got distracted. She wandered off, and by the time I realized she was gone, it was too late."

His voice broke, and he paused to collect himself. Emma's heart broke for him, her own eyes filling with tears. "Joseph, it wasn't your fault."

He shook his head, tears glistening in his eyes. "It was, Emma. I should have been paying attention. I should have kept her safe. When we found her... she had fallen through the ice on the pond. I couldn't save her."

Emma's grip on his arm tightened, her own tears spilling over. "Joseph, you were just a boy. You can't blame yourself for what happened. It was a tragic accident."

"She drowned, Emma. It was a day just like this, and I was too excited for Christmas to take care of her properly. I thought — I thought she would be okay, and so I let her go outside on her own. I—" he choked, tears threatening to spill.

"Oh, Joseph…"

Joseph wiped at his eyes, his expression haunted. "I've carried that guilt with me every day. Every Christmas, it all comes flooding back. I see her face, hear her laughter... and then I remember how I failed her."

Emma moved closer, wrapping her arms around him in a comforting embrace. The cold of the barn was almost forgotten in their shared warmth. "Joseph, you didn't fail her. You loved her, and you did everything you could. Sometimes, terrible things happen, and we can't control them."

He leaned into her embrace, his body shaking with silent sobs. The wind outside continued to howl, but inside the barn, there was a moment of stillness. "I just wish I could go back and change things."

Emma held him tighter, her heart breaking for the pain he carried. "I know, Joseph. Ruth wouldn't want you to live with this guilt. She would want you to remember the happy times, to find peace and forgiveness."

Joseph slowly pulled back, looking into her eyes with a mixture of gratitude and sorrow. "Thank you, Emma. You have no idea how much it means to hear you say that."

She smiled softly, her hand gently brushing a tear from his cheek. "You're strong, Joseph. Stronger than you know. You have a good heart. Ruth would be proud of you."

Joseph took a shaky breath, the tears still glistening in his eyes but his expression calmer. "I've never really talked about it with anyone, not even my parents. They were so devastated. I felt like I had to carry the burden alone."

Emma nodded, understanding the weight of his silence. "Sometimes sharing our pain can help lighten the load. I'm glad you told me, Joseph."

He managed a small, grateful smile. "It feels like a small weight has been lifted, just by talking about it."

Emma squeezed his hand. "I'm here for you, Joseph. Always."

They sat there for a while longer, the storm continuing to rage outside but the atmosphere inside the barn growing warmer with their shared understanding. The connection between them felt stronger than ever, bound by trust.

The wind continued to howl, but it seemed a bit less menacing now. Emma leaned her head against Joseph's shoulder, feeling a sense of peace despite the storm. She knew that they still had much to talk about, but for now, being together was enough.

As the hours passed, they huddled close for warmth, their breaths mingling in the cold air. The barn provided minimal shelter, but their shared body heat kept the worst of the chill at bay. Emma listened to the rhythm of Joseph's breathing, finding comfort in his presence.

Eventually, the storm began to subside, the howling wind dying down to a low murmur. The quiet after the storm felt almost surreal, a sharp contrast to the chaos they had endured.

Joseph stirred, his voice a soft whisper in the dim light. "The storm seems to be letting up. We should find the horses as soon as it's safe."

Emma nodded, feeling a mixture of relief and lingering worry. "Yes, we should, but let's wait a little longer, just to be sure."

They remained huddled together, listening to the gentle sounds of the barn and the faint rustle of the wind outside. The fear and cold of the storm had brought them closer, and Emma felt a renewed sense of determination. She would face whatever came next with Joseph by her side.

When they finally stepped outside, the world was transformed. The storm had left a thick blanket of snow covering everything, turning the landscape into a winter wonderland. The air was crisp and clear, the clouds filling the sky as the sun tried to emerge above a cloud.

It didn't take long to find the missing horses. They were huddled together under a large tree not far from the barn, their breaths visible in the frigid air. Relief flooded Emma as she and Joseph approached them, speaking soothingly to calm their nerves.

"You're all right," Joseph murmured, stroking the neck of one of the horses. "We're here now."

Emma did the same, feeling the warmth of the horse's body against her hand. "Let's get them back to the farm. They'll be safe and warm there."

They led the horses back home, their steps careful on the icy ground. By the time they arrived, the sun was beginning to break through the clouds, casting a soft golden light over the snow-covered fields. Abram and Maria met them at the gate, their faces filled with relief and gratitude.

"Thank Gott you're all safe," Abram said, his voice choked with emotion. "I was so worried."

Emma smiled, her heart light. "We're fine, I promise. The horses are, too."

As they settled the horses back into the barn, Emma felt a new sense of clarity. The time she had spent with Joseph during the storm, seeing his vulnerability and strength, had solidified her feelings. She knew now that she wanted to give their relationship a real chance.

Later that evening, after they had all warmed up and shared a hearty meal, Emma found a quiet moment to speak with Joseph. They stood by the window, watching the sun set over the snowy landscape.

"Joseph," Emma began, her voice soft but steady, "I've been thinking a lot about us. About everything that's happened."

He turned to her, his expression open and hopeful. "What have you decided?"

Emma took a deep breath, her heart pounding with anticipation. "I want to give us a chance. I want to go to the pageant with you, and see where this leads."

Joseph's face lit up with a smile that warmed her from the inside out. "Emma, that means more to me than you can imagine."

She smiled back, feeling a weight lift from her shoulders. "Thank you for giving me a second chance."

The decision made, the atmosphere in the room felt lighter. They both stood by the window, enjoying the serene beauty of the snow-covered fields as the last rays of sunlight painted the sky in hues of pink and gold.

Abram entered the room, his gaze shifting between Emma and Joseph. "Everything all right?" he asked, a hint of concern in his voice.

Emma nodded, her smile reassuring. "Yes, Daed. Everything is all right."

Joseph echoed her sentiment. "We've decided to go to the pageant together."

Abram's eyes softened with understanding and approval. "I'm glad to hear that. It's good to see you both moving forward."

After Abram left, they continued to stand in comfortable silence, absorbing the tranquility of the moment. Emma felt an overwhelming sense of gratitude for the support of her family and the promise of a new beginning with Joseph.

The next day dawned clear and bright, the storm a mere memory. The farm was bustling with activity as they prepared for the upcoming festivities. Emma's heart was light as she moved through her chores, the conversation with Joseph giving her a renewed sense of purpose and joy.

As the day of the Christmas pageant approached, excitement and anticipation filled the air. The community center was decorated beautifully, with warm glowing candles and festive garlands adorning every corner. Emma and Joseph arrived together, their hands entwined, their hearts aligned in a shared hope for the future.

Chapter Eight

Joseph's heart pounded with a mix of excitement and nerves as he and Emma walked hand in hand toward the church. The air was crisp and cold, the night sky clear and filled with stars. The entire community had gathered for the Christmas Eve service, a cherished tradition that brought everyone together in celebration and reflection.

As they entered the warmly lit church, Joseph felt a wave of anticipation. Tonight was the night he and Emma had decided to make their intentions known. The decision to court had come naturally after their deep conversations and the shared moments of vulnerability during the storm. Now, they were ready to take the next step together.

The service was beautiful, filled with hymns and prayers that touched Joseph's soul. He felt a deep sense of gratitude for the blessings in his life, particularly for Emma, who stood beside him, her presence a constant source of strength and comfort. As the final hymn echoed through the church, he glanced at her, finding reassurance in her serene expression.

After the service, the congregation mingled outside the church, exchanging warm wishes and enjoying the festive atmosphere. The time had come. Joseph took a deep breath and looked at Emma, who nodded encouragingly. Together, they approached their parents, who were standing in a small circle, chatting amicably.

"Daed, Mamm," Emma began, her voice steady but filled with emotion. "Joseph and I have something we'd like to share with you."

Maria and Abram turned to her, curiosity and warmth in their eyes. "What is it, love?" Abram asked.

Joseph's parents, Martha and John, who had been standing nearby, also turned their attention to the young couple, sensing the significance of the moment.

Joseph exchanged a quick glance with Emma, who squeezed his hand for support. "Emma and I have decided to court," he announced, his voice clear and confident.

"We wanted to share our intentions with you tonight, on Christmas Eve, surrounded by our family and community."

For a moment, there was silence as their parents absorbed the news. Then, smiles broke out on their faces, and tears of joy glistened in Maria's eyes.

"Oh, Emma, Joseph," Maria said, her voice choked with emotion. "This is wonderful news."

Martha pulled her son into a warm embrace. "We're so happy for you both," she said, her eyes shining with pride and happiness.

Abram clapped Joseph on the shoulder, his grip firm and reassuring. "I knew you two were meant for each other. This is a blessed day."

John nodded in agreement, his expression one of deep satisfaction. "You've made us very proud. May Gott bless your courtship."

The happiness and approval from their parents filled Joseph's heart with warmth and gratitude. He looked at Emma, who was beaming with joy, and felt a profound sense of rightness about their decision.

As their families continued to share in the celebration, Joseph gently pulled Emma aside. They stood under a canopy of twinkling stars, the crisp air filled with the sounds of laughter and joy from the gathered community.

"Emma," Joseph said softly, taking both her hands in his. "I'm so grateful for you, for us. This moment feels like the start of something truly special."

Emma smiled, her eyes sparkling with happiness. "It does, Joseph. I'm so glad we're on this journey together."

In the glow of the church lights and the festive decorations, Joseph leaned in and pressed a chaste, tender kiss on Emma's lips. It was a promise, a beginning, and a celebration all in one simple gesture. The kiss was brief but filled with all the love and hope they felt for their future together.

As they pulled back, Emma's cheeks were rosy, and her smile was radiant. Joseph felt a surge of happiness, knowing that they had the support of their families and the blessing of their community.

***

After the church service, both families decided to walk back to the Fisher farm together. The moonlight illuminated their path, making the snow sparkle like a sea of diamonds. Joseph walked beside Emma, their hands intertwined, while their parents followed closely behind, chatting and laughing.

"It's a beautiful night," Maria remarked, her breath forming clouds in the cold air.

"It truly is," Abram agreed, looking up at the clear, star-studded sky. "A perfect night to celebrate such wonderful news."

Martha smiled warmly. "We couldn't be happier for Joseph and Emma. They make such a lovely couple."

John nodded, his expression thoughtful. "It's a blessing to see our children find happiness. They have strong hearts and good heads on their shoulders."

The group continued their walk, the conversation flowing easily between them. Joseph squeezed Emma's hand gently, feeling a deep sense of contentment as they neared the farmhouse. The warm lights spilling from the windows were a welcoming sight, promising comfort and celebration.

Inside, the house was filled with festive decorations. A simple but beautifully decorated Christmas tree stood in the corner of the living room, adorned with handmade ornaments and strings of popcorn. Candles flickered on the mantel, casting a warm glow over the room.

"Let's get settled in and enjoy our meal," Maria said, ushering everyone to the table.

The large wooden table was laden with an array of Christmas dishes. There was roasted goose, its skin golden and crisp, surrounded by roasted root vegetables. A basket of freshly baked bread rolls sat next to a bowl of creamy mashed potatoes. There were also jars of pickled beets, homemade applesauce, and a large dish of green beans cooked with bacon.

As everyone took their seats, Emma felt a deep sense of contentment. She was surrounded by family and the man she cared about, ready to celebrate the joy of the season together.

"Let's say grace," Abram suggested, bowing his head. The room fell silent as he led them in a heartfelt prayer, thanking Gott for the blessings of the year and asking for guidance and protection for the coming days.

After the prayer, the lively conversation resumed. Plates were passed around, and soon everyone was enjoying the delicious feast.

"This bread is amazing, Maria," Martha praised, breaking off a piece of the warm roll. "You must share your recipe with me."

Maria laughed softly. "Of course, Martha. It's an old family recipe, handed down through generations."

As the meal progressed, the room was filled with laughter and stories. John and Abram reminisced about their own childhood Christmases, sharing tales of mischief and tradition that brought smiles to everyone's faces.

"I remember one year," John began, "we decided to build the biggest snowman our village had ever seen. We spent the whole day rolling the snow, and by the end, it was taller than the barn!"

Abram chuckled. "And then it toppled over just as you were putting the hat on it, didn't it?"

John nodded, grinning. "That's right. It was quite the spectacle."

Joseph leaned in to Emma, whispering, "I love hearing these old stories. It makes me feel connected to our roots."

Emma smiled, squeezing his hand. "Me too. It's what makes our traditions so special."

As the evening went on, the conversations shifted to the future. Plans for the coming year, hopes, and dreams were shared around the table.

"What are your plans for the farm next year, Abram?" John asked, taking a sip of his apple cider.

"We're hoping to expand the vegetable garden," Abram replied. "Maybe add a few more chickens to the coop. Emma has been a great help with the planning."

Maria added, "And we're looking forward to seeing what new ideas Joseph and Emma bring as they start this new chapter together."

Martha nodded, her eyes warm with approval. "It's wonderful to see our families coming together. The future looks bright."

As the meal came to an end, Maria brought out a platter of Christmas cookies and a warm apple pie, its sweet aroma filling the room.

Emma happily ate the pie, enjoying the warmth and sweetness. Everyone continued to talk, but she was content to sit and listen.

As the night drew to a close, Joseph and Emma found a quiet moment together. They stood by the window, looking out at the snow-covered landscape, the moonlight casting a gentle glow over the scene.

"Tonight has been perfect," Emma said softly, leaning her head on Joseph's shoulder.

"It has," Joseph agreed, wrapping his arm around her. "It's just the beginning. I can't wait to see what the future holds for us."

Emma smiled, feeling a sense of peace and joy. They had faced challenges and uncertainties, but tonight was a testament to the strength of their love and the support of their families.

After a while, Emma and Joseph slipped outside for a few moments of solitude under the stars. The cold air was crisp, and their breath formed small clouds as they spoke.

"I'm so happy we made our intentions known tonight," Joseph said, his eyes shining with emotion. "It feels like a weight has been lifted."

Emma nodded, her heart full. "I'm glad too. Sharing it with our families and seeing their joy made it even more special. On Christmas, too!"

Joseph took both of her hands in his, his touch warm against the chill. "Emma, I promise to always be by your side, to support and cherish you."

Tears of happiness welled up in Emma's eyes as she looked into his. "I'm only sorry it took me so long to know how I feel."

In the stillness of the winter night, under the canopy of stars, they shared a tender, chaste kiss, sealing their promises with a gesture that spoke volumes of their love and commitment.

As they re-joined their families inside, the warmth of the home and the joy of the evening enveloped them. The night was filled with celebration and joy, a perfect start to their journey as a couple, supported by the love and faith of their community.

Chapter Nine

Emma and Joseph spent time together in the winter months, enjoying simple activities like sledding and ice skating. One crisp Saturday afternoon, they found themselves at the top of a gentle hill near the farm, a pair of sleds ready for use. The air was filled with the quiet sounds of winter—the crunch of snow underfoot, the occasional chirp of a bird, and the distant bark of a dog.

"Are you ready, Emma?" Joseph asked, his eyes sparkling with excitement.

Emma laughed, adjusting her scarf. "Ready as I'll ever be. Let's go!"

With a push, they launched themselves down the hill, the cold wind whipping past their faces. Emma's laughter echoed through the air, mingling with Joseph's. The thrill of the descent made her heart race, and for a moment, all her worries melted away.

At the bottom of the hill, they tumbled off their sleds, breathless and laughing. Joseph helped Emma to her feet, his grip warm and steady despite the chill in the air.

"That was amazing!" Emma exclaimed, brushing snow from her coat.

"Let's do it again," Joseph suggested, his enthusiasm infectious.

They spent the afternoon sledding, each run down the hill filled with more laughter and shared joy. When they finally grew tired, they decided to take a walk through the snowy fields, the sun beginning to dip toward the horizon.

As they walked, their breaths visible in the cold air, they talked about their future dreams and aspirations. Emma found herself opening up to Joseph in ways she hadn't before, sharing her hopes for the farm and her desire to build a strong, loving family.

"I want to create a place where everyone feels welcome," Emma said, her voice thoughtful. "A home filled with love and laughter."

Joseph nodded, his expression serious. "I feel the same way. I want to work the land, to provide for my family, and to be a good husband and father."

Emma's heart warmed at his words. "I believe you will be, Joseph. You're one of the kindest, most hardworking people I know."

He smiled, a soft blush coloring his cheeks. "Really? I had no idea you felt so strongly."

She smiled, and pressed a kiss to the side of his jaw. "Of course, I love you."

***

In the evenings, Emma and Joseph attended community gatherings, where their growing affection for each other became more evident to those around them. One such evening, they joined a group of friends and neighbors for a potluck dinner at the community center. The room was filled with the warm glow of lanterns and the rich aroma of home-cooked food.

As they entered, Joseph placed a gentle hand on Emma's back, guiding her through the crowd. They were greeted with smiles and warm wishes, the community's support palpable.

"Emma, Joseph! Over here!" called out Catherine.

They made their way to the table, greeting friends along the way. The conversation flowed easily, filled with laughter and shared stories. Emma couldn't help but notice the approving glances and whispered comments from those around them.

"Looks like you two are quite the pair," Catherine said with a wink, nudging Emma playfully.

Emma blushed, glancing at Joseph. "We're very happy," she admitted, her smile genuine.

Joseph nodded, his eyes meeting Emma's with warmth. "It's true. I feel very blessed."

Throughout the evening, they were surrounded by friends and family who expressed their excitement and support for their budding relationship. The sense of community and belonging filled Emma's heart with gratitude and joy.

***

As their courtship progressed, Emma and Joseph found themselves having more conversations with friends and family about their future plans. One Sunday afternoon, they sat with Emma's parents, Maria and Abram, in the cozy living room of the farmhouse.

"Joseph, Emma," Abram began, his tone serious but kind. "Your mother and I have been talking, and we wanted to know more about your plans. What are your thoughts for the future?"

Joseph took a deep breath, his hand finding Emma's. "Mr. Fisher, Mrs. Fisher, Emma and I have been discussing our dreams and goals. We want to build a life together, one that honors our families and our faith."

Maria smiled warmly. "That sounds wonderful. We have always hoped for a future filled with love and happiness for both of you."

Emma squeezed Joseph's hand, feeling a sense of unity. "We plan to continue working on the farm, to expand and improve it. We want to create a home that welcomes everyone, just like you and Daed have done."

Abram nodded approvingly. "Those are good plans. It's clear that you both have thought this through."

Later, they visited Joseph's parents, Martha and John, sharing similar conversations. Martha's eyes shone with pride as she listened to their plans.

"You have our full support," Martha said, her voice filled with emotion. "It's wonderful to see how deeply you care for each other."

John clapped Joseph on the shoulder. "You've grown into a fine young man, Joseph. We're proud of you, and we're excited for your future with Emma."

With each conversation, the community's support and excitement for their relationship grew. Emma and Joseph felt a deep sense of gratitude for the love and encouragement that surrounded them.

As the winter months passed, their bond strengthened, and the future looked brighter with each passing day. Emma and Joseph knew that, together, they could face any challenge and build a life filled with love, joy, and purpose.

***

Spring arrived in full bloom, and Emma and Joseph found themselves basking in the beauty of the season. The days were longer, the air warmer, and the world around them seemed to burst with new life. One bright afternoon, they decided to take a break from their work and enjoy a picnic by the stream that ran through the edge of the Fisher farm.

They packed a simple meal—fresh bread, cheese, and fruit—along with a blanket and set off hand in hand. The walk to the stream was filled with the sounds of birds singing and the gentle rustle of leaves in the breeze. Wildflowers dotted the path, their vibrant colors a testament to the promise of spring.

When they reached their favorite spot by the stream, they spread out the blanket and sat down, the sun casting a warm glow over them. The water sparkled in the light, creating a peaceful and picturesque scene.

"This is perfect," Emma said, leaning back on her elbows and looking up at the clear blue sky. "I love this time of year."

Joseph smiled, his heart swelling with contentment. "So do I. It's like everything is starting fresh, full of hope and possibilities."

They ate their meal slowly, savoring the flavors and the tranquility of the moment. Emma plucked a wildflower and tucked it behind her ear, a playful smile on her lips.

"You look beautiful," Joseph said, reaching out to gently touch the flower. "Spring suits you."

Emma blushed, her eyes twinkling with happiness. "Thank you, Joseph. I feel so blessed to be sharing this with you."

After their meal, they lay back on the blanket, side by side, watching the clouds drift lazily across the sky. The world seemed to slow down, allowing them to fully appreciate the simple joy of being together.

"Do you ever think about the future, Emma?" Joseph asked, his voice soft and reflective.

"All the time," Emma replied, turning her head to look at him. "I think about the home we'll build, the family we'll raise, and the life we'll share. It makes me so happy to imagine it all."

Joseph nodded, a peaceful smile on his face. "Me too. I know we'll face challenges, but with you by my side, I feel like we can handle anything."

Emma reached out and intertwined her fingers with his, their hands resting between them. "We'll face everything together, Joseph. That's all that matters."

As the afternoon sun began to lower in the sky, casting long shadows over the meadow, they decided to visit the local market. The market was bustling with activity, filled with stalls of fresh produce, handmade crafts, and the delicious aroma of baked goods.

They wandered through the stalls, sampling treats and admiring the various wares. Joseph bought a small wooden carving of a bird for Emma, a symbol of their shared love for nature and the simple beauty of life.

"This is lovely, Joseph," Emma said, holding the carving gently. "Thank you."

He smiled, pleased by her reaction. "I'm glad you like it. It reminded me of you."

As they continued to explore the market, they ran into friends and neighbors who greeted them warmly. Mary, a close friend of Emma's, stopped to chat, her eyes bright with excitement.

"You two look so happy," Mary said, her smile wide. "It's wonderful to see."

"We are," Emma replied, glancing at Joseph. "Every day feels like a blessing."

The market visit ended with them sharing a warm, freshly baked pie, sitting on a bench and watching the world go by. The simple pleasures of the day filled them with a sense of peace and fulfillment.

As they walked back home, hand in hand, the setting sun painted the sky with hues of pink and gold. The promise of spring and the warmth of their love wrapped around them like a comforting blanket.

"This has been such a wonderful day," Emma said softly, leaning into Joseph as they walked.

As they approached the farmhouse, the lights glowing warmly in the gathering dusk, they knew that their journey together was just beginning, filled with hope, love, and the promise of many more beautiful days to come.

Epilogue

The morning of Emma and Joseph's wedding dawned clear and crisp, with the air filled with the scent of fallen leaves and the promise of a new beginning. The sun cast a warm golden glow over the farm, making the snow-covered fields sparkle. Emma woke up with a flutter of excitement in her chest, her heart filled with joy and anticipation.

She dressed in a simple yet beautiful gown, handmade with love by her mother, Maria. The dress was modest, as was customary, made of soft ivory fabric that flowed gracefully. Her hair was braided and adorned with a delicate lace cap, a traditional

Amish accessory that symbolized purity and commitment.

As Emma looked at herself in the mirror, she felt a sense of calm wash over her. This was the day she had dreamed of, a day filled with love and the promise of a shared future with Joseph.

"Emma, you look beautiful," Maria said, her eyes misting with tears as she adjusted the lace cap on her daughter's head. "I'm so proud of you."

"Thank you, Mamm," Emma replied, hugging her mother tightly. "I'm so happy."

The wedding ceremony was held in the community church, a simple but elegant building filled with friends and family. The pews were adorned with fresh flowers and greenery, and the soft glow of candles added to the warm atmosphere.

Joseph stood at the front of the church, dressed in a traditional black suit and white shirt. His eyes shone with love and admiration as he watched Emma walk down the aisle, escorted by her father, Abram. The soft rustle of her dress and the quiet whispers of the guests filled the air.

As Emma reached the front of the church, Abram gently placed her hand in Joseph's. The moment felt sacred as she gazed up at her soon to be husband.

The bishop began the ceremony with a prayer, asking for Gott's blessing on their union. "Dear Gott, we ask for your guidance and blessing as Emma and Joseph join their lives together. May their love grow stronger with each passing day, and may they find joy and fulfillment in their shared journey."

Emma and Joseph stood before the bishop, their hands clasped together. The vows they spoke were simple but filled with deep emotion, reflecting their commitment to each other and to their faith.

"Emma," Joseph began, his voice steady and filled with love, "I promise to be your faithful husband, to love and honor you, and to stand by your side through all the days of our lives. With Gott's guidance, I will strive to be a husband worthy of your love and trust."

Tears welled up in Emma's eyes as she replied, "Joseph, I promise to be your faithful wife, to love and support you, and to walk with you in faith and devotion. With Gott's help, I will be a wife worthy of your love and commitment."

The bishop then led them through the vows, which included promises to uphold their faith, to work together in harmony, and to build a home filled with love and grace. The simplicity and sincerity of the vows resonated deeply with everyone present.

With the exchange of vows complete, the bishop pronounced them husband and wife. "By the authority given to me by Gott and this community, I declare you, Joseph and Emma, to be husband and wife. May your lives be filled with joy, love, and peace."

Joseph and Emma turned to face their family and friends, their faces radiant with happiness. As they shared their first kiss as husband and wife, the church erupted in applause and joyful cheers. The kiss was tender and filled with promise, a symbol of their deep love and the bright future they would build together.

"I love you, Emma," Joseph whispered as they parted, his eyes shining with emotion.

"I love you too, Joseph," Emma replied, her heart overflowing with happiness.

After the ceremony, everyone gathered at the Fisher farm for the wedding feast. Long tables were set up in the barn, decorated with simple but beautiful centerpieces of wildflowers and candles. The aroma of roasted meats, fresh bread, and sweet desserts filled the air, making mouths water in anticipation.

The meal was a traditional Amish feast, featuring dishes like roast chicken, mashed potatoes, green beans, and homemade pies. The guests ate heartily, the barn filled with the sounds of laughter, conversation, and the clinking of plates and glasses.

Emma and Joseph sat at the head of the table, surrounded by their closest family and friends. As they enjoyed the meal, they shared stories and memories, their love for each other evident in every glance and touch.

After the meal, the celebration continued with singing and dancing. The children played games in the yard, their laughter echoing through the night. The adults joined in the dances, their movements joyful and full of life.

As the evening drew to a close, Emma and Joseph slipped away for a moment of quiet reflection. They stood together in the cool night air, looking up at the stars that filled the sky.

"This has been the most perfect day," Emma said softly, her hand resting on Joseph's arm.

"It has," Joseph agreed, pulling her close. "I can't wait to spend my life with you."

They shared another kiss, the promise of their love and commitment as bright and eternal as the stars above. As they stood there, wrapped in each other's arms, they knew that no matter what the future held, they would face it together, with faith, love, and the support of their community.

Printed in Great Britain
by Amazon